To my wonderful agent, Karen.
Thank you for helping me share my
burgeoning words with the world.
—J. B. -W.

For Stephen x
—S. H.

Published by
PEACHTREE PUBLISHING COMPANY INC.
1700 Chattahoochee Avenue
Atlanta, Georgia 30318-2112
PeachtreeBooks.com

Text © 2023 by JaNay Brown-Wood
Illustrations © 2023 by Samara Hardy

Designed by Adela Pons
Edited by Jonah Heller

The illustrations were created in Photoshop using
layers of hand-painted ink and watercolor textures.

Printed and bound in November 2022 at Toppan
Leefung, DongGuan, China.
10 9 8 7 6 5 4 3 2 1
First Edition
ISBN: 978-1-68263-168-3

Cataloging-in-Publication Data
is available from the Library
of Congress.

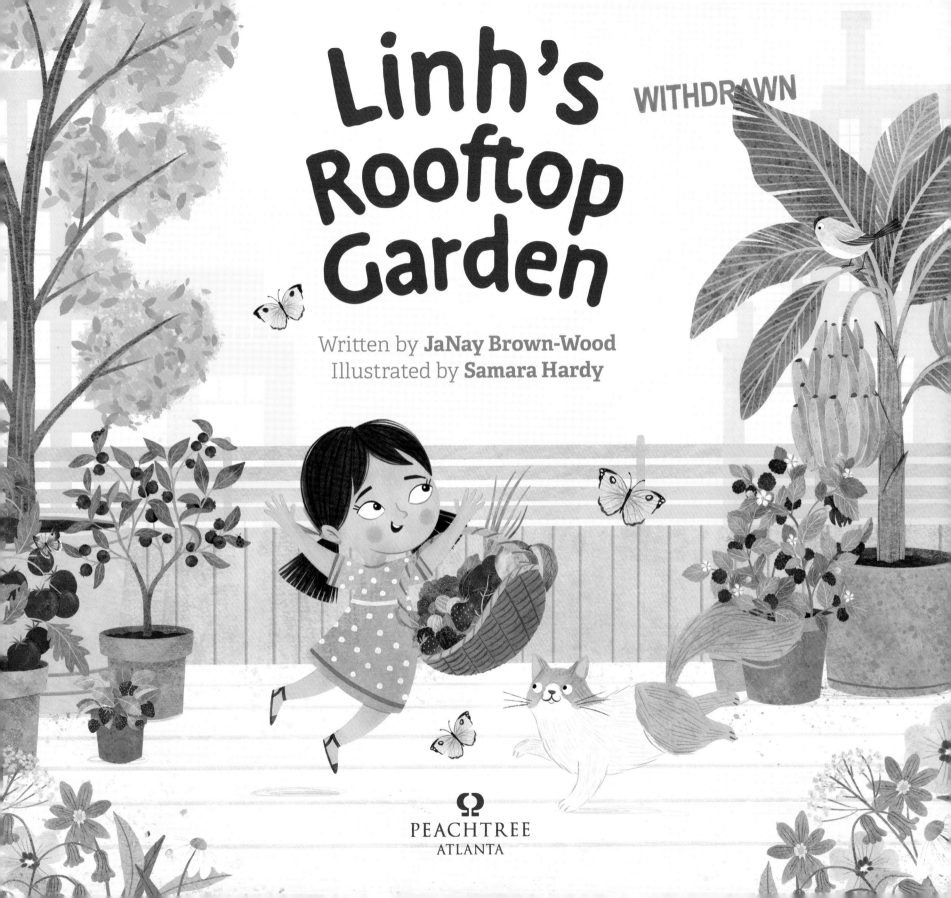

Linh's Rooftop Garden

Written by **JaNay Brown-Wood**

Illustrated by **Samara Hardy**

PEACHTREE

ATLANTA

Linh has many plants on her rooftop garden.

Today, Linh must find her **blueberries** for her family brunch party. What do we know about **blueberries**?

A blueberry . . .

is small, blue, and round in shape
with a thin skin that can be eaten.

It has pointy edges on the top that
form a crown, and a pale green inside,
with many seeds in the center.

It also grows in bunches on bushes,
hanging on by thin green stems
among waxy pointed leaves with
smooth edges.

Let's help Linh find her blueberries!

A **blueberry** is small and blue.
Is that a **blueberry**?

No. Those are gooseberries.
A gooseberry is small, and it can
be many different colors like
purple, white, black, green,
and red—but not blue!

A **blueberry** is round in shape.
Is that a **blueberry**?

No. Those are blackberries. A blackberry does have round balls all over it, but those balls usually bunch together to form a cone shape.

A **blueberry** has a thin skin that can be eaten. Is that a **blueberry**?

No. Those are onions. An onion does have a thin skin, but its skin is peeled away and not eaten.

A **blueberry** has pointy edges on top that form a crown. Is that a **blueberry**?

No. That's broccoli. Broccoli does have a crown, but its crown is bushy like a tiny tree and not pointy.

A **blueberry** has a pale green inside.
Is that a **blueberry**?

No. Those are tomatoes. A tomato can have a pale green inside, but its insides are mostly red when ripe and ready to eat.

A blueberry has many seeds in the center. Is that a blueberry?

No. Those are raspberries. A raspberry has many seeds, but its seeds are spread all around instead of right in the center.

A blueberry grows in bunches on bushes. Is that a blueberry?

No. Those are bananas. Bananas do grow in bunches, but they grow on trees—not on bushes.

A **blueberry** hangs from its
bush by a thin green stem.
Is that a **blueberry**?

No. Those are peaches. A peach
does hang down by a stem, but its
stem is brown and thicker than a
blueberry stem.

A blueberry grows among waxy pointed leaves with smooth edges. Is that a blueberry?

No. Those are strawberries. A strawberry grows among leaves, but its leaves are not waxy and have many jagged points.

Linh's family brunch party won't be
perfect without her **blueberries.**

We've searched and searched and still no luck!

Where, where, *where* can they be?

Are those blueberries?

Why, yes!
Those are **blueberries!**

They are small, blue, and round in shape with a thin skin that can be eaten. They have crowns on top with pointy edges, pale green insides, and many seeds in their center. And they grow in bunches on bushes from thin green stems, among waxy pointed leaves with smooth edges.

Hooray!

We've found Linh's blueberries.

And just in time for some scrumptious treats!

Which produce can *you* find at Linh's family brunch party?

Blueberry and Banana Pancakes

2–4 Servings

Ingredients

- 2 ripe bananas
- ½ cup blueberries
- ¼ tsp cinnamon
- 2 eggs
- ½ cup uncooked instant oats
- 1 tsp vanilla extract
- Pinch of salt
- Butter or cooking spray (optional)
- Pancake syrup
- Chopped pecans

Directions

1. Wash all your produce in warm water.
2. Crack eggs into separate bowl and set aside for later.
3. Snap off the top of your bananas and peel them, then put them into a bowl.
4. Mash bananas until they are nice and smooth.
5. Measure out the vanilla and cinnamon and add each ingredient to the mashed bananas, stirring thoroughly. Then, add a pinch of salt.
6. Mix in the previously cracked eggs.
7. Add instant oats and stir until oats are fully moistened.
8. Carefully fold in the blueberries using a wooden spoon or plastic spatula.
9. After the batter is prepared, ask your adult helper to heat a griddle or skillet to medium heat.
10. Have adult helper add a little butter or cooking spray and scoop out ¼ cup of batter, then smooth out batter with spatula so it is even.
11. With the help of your adult, cook the pancake for 2–3 minutes and when you see bubbles, flip it to cook the other side for about 1–2 minutes more. Remove from pan and set aside. Repeat steps 10–11 until all batter is used.
12. Stack desired number of pancakes on dish, then top with syrup and chopped pecans.
13. Enjoy!

You'll also need: 1 trusty adult helper